Date: 10/20/16

J GRA 741.5 FIG V.5
Zub, Jim,
Figment. Journey into imagination

PALM BEACH COUNTY
LIBRARY SYSTEM
3650 SUMMIT BLVD.
WEST PALM BEACH, FL 33406

FIGMENT

JOURNEY INTO IMAGINATION, VOLUME 5

ABDO Spotlight   Disney KINGDOMS   MARVEL

ABDOPUBLISHING.COM

Reinforced library bound edition published in 2016 by Spotlight,
a division of ABDO, PO Box 398166, Minneapolis, Minnesota 55439.
Spotlight produces high-quality reinforced library bound editions for
schools and libraries. Published by agreement with Marvel Characters, Inc.

Printed in the United States of America, North Mankato, Minnesota.
092015
012016

THIS BOOK CONTAINS
RECYCLED MATERIALS

MARVEL
marvelkids.com
© 2016 MARVEL

Elements based on Figment © Disney.

CATALOGING-IN-PUBLICATION DATA

Zub, Jim.
 Figment : journey into imagination / writer, Jim Zub ; artist, Filipe Andrade
and John Tyler Christopher. -- Reinforced library bound edition.
   p. cm. (Figment : journey into imagination)
"Marvel."
Summary: Dive into a steampunk fantasy story exploring the never-before-
revealed origin of the inventor known as Dreamfinder, and how one little
spark of inspiration created a dragon called Figment.
ISBN 978-1-61479-445-5 (vol. 1) -- ISBN 978-1-61479-446-2 (vol. 2) -- ISBN
978-1-61479-447-9 (vol. 3) -- ISBN 978-1-61479-448-6 (vol. 4) -- ISBN 978-1-
61479-449-3 (vol. 5)
1. Figment (Fictitious character)--Juvenile fiction. 2. Dragons--Juvenile
fiction. 3. Adventure and adventures--Juvenile fiction. 4. Graphic novels-
-Juvenile fiction. I. Andrade, Filipe, illustrator. II. Christopher, John Tyler,
illustrator. III. Title.
741.5--dc23

2015955126

Spotlight

A Division of ABDO
abdopublishing.com

Journey Into Imagination
Part Five

JIM ZUB writer
FILIPE ANDRADE artist
JEAN-FRANCOIS BEAULIEU colorist
VC'S JOE CARAMAGNA letterer

JOHN TYLER CHRISTOPHER cover artist

**JIM CLARK, BRIAN CROSBY,
ANDY DIGENOVA, TOM MORRIS
& JOSH SHIPLEY**
walt disney imagineers

MARK BASSO assistant editor
BILL ROSEMANN editor

AXEL ALONSO editor in chief
JOE QUESADA chief creative officer
DAN BUCKLEY publisher

special thanks to
DAVID GABRIEL

WOOSH

Farewell, Figment Faithful!

I know it's a groan-worthy cliché, but I can't help it – Working on FIGMENT has been a dream come true!

Right from the start – from concept, through development, and then into art production and lettering – everyone on the team clicked. All of us gathered momentum and enthusiasm as the project built up steam. I think that creative 'spark' really shows on the final printed page, each one lovingly rendered by Filipe Andrade and Jean-Francois Beaulieu.

Expanding the legacy of Dreamfinder and Figment has been a magical experience all around. I know how much these characters mean to fans of Walt Disney World and I'm delighted that you've welcomed this new story into your hearts.

To the creative team, the Marvel crew, the Disney Imagineers, and our loyal readers – Thank you for letting me add a bit of steam-powered joy to the Magic Kingdom.

-Jim Zub

What can I say? Comics should be fun, and this book had it in spades. I had an absolute blast during our journey, and working with this team has been nothing but pleasant. A sincere thank you to the entire creative team, as well as to the fans and readers. I hope you had as much fun reading this series as I had coloring it—because, remember, comics should be fun!

-Jean-Francois Beaulieu

Thank you for joining us on this imaginative journey...and stay tuned for news on our next great Disney Kingdoms adventure!
-Bill Rosemann

© Disney

**Early Figment and Dreamfinder character designs
for the Journey Into Imagination ride by X Atencio**

Artwork courtesy of Walt Disney Imagineering Art Collection